D0160645

The Bridesmaid Ballet

Katharine Holabird

Illustrated by Chris Russell

Based on the original artwork by Helen Craig

Grosset & Dunlap

To my lovely nieces, Melinda, Olivia, and Emma—
with tons of love

GROSSET & DUNLAP
Published by the Penguin Group
Penguin Group (USA) Inc., 375 Hudson Street, New York, New York 10014, U.S.A.
Penguin Group (Canada), 90 Eglinton Avenue East, Suite 700, Toronto, Ontario, Canada M4P 2Y3
(a division of Pearson Penguin Canada Inc.)
Penguin Books Ltd, 80 Strand, London WC2R 0RL, England
Penguin Ireland, 25 St Stephen's Green, Dublin 2, Ireland
(a division of Penguin Books Ltd)
Penguin Group (Australia), 250 Camberwell Road, Camberwell, Victoria 3124, Australia
(a division of Pearson Australia Group Pty Ltd)
Penguin Books India Pvt Ltd, 11 Community Centre, Panchsheel Park, New Delhi - 110 017, India
Penguin Group (NZ), Cnr Airborne and Rosedale Roads, Albany, Auckland 1310, New Zealand
(a division of Pearson New Zealand Ltd)
Penguin Books (South Africa) (Pty) Ltd, 24 Sturdee Avenue, Rosebank, Johannesburg 2196, South Africa

Penguin Books Ltd, Registered Offices:
80 Strand, London WC2R 0RL, England

First published in Great Britain 2006 by Puffin Books.

Angelina Ballerina © 2006 Helen Craig Ltd. and Katharine Holabird. The Angelina Ballerina
name and character and the dancing Angelina logo are trademarks of HIT Entertainment Ltd.,
Katharine Holabird, and Helen Craig. Reg. U.S. Pat. & Tm. Off. Used under license by
Penguin Young Readers Group. All rights reserved. Published by Grosset & Dunlap,
a division of Penguin Young Readers Group, 345 Hudson Street, New York, New York 10014.
GROSSET & DUNLAP is a trademark of Penguin Group (USA) Inc. Printed in the U.S.A.

Library of Congress Control Number: 2006011384

ISBN 0-448-44386-4   10 9 8 7 6 5 4 3 2 1

Dear Diary,

I have a truly ginormous wish—I would soooo LOVE to be a bridesmaid! I can't wait to be invited to a gorgeous wedding.

. . . I'll need a special bridesmaid dress and shiny ribbons and dancing slippers and a wreath of flowers in my fur. Imagine!

My very bestest friend, Alice, agrees with me. She says that bridesmaids are the best thing since cheddar cheese!

After school today, Alice and I skipped home to Honeysuckle Cottage together and clambered up the old oak tree at the bottom of my garden. Alice was giggling with excitement as I opened the creaky door of our Treetop Club.

"So what's the big surprise, Angelina?" she asked as we plopped down on our comfy cushions. I poured two glasses of pink lemonade and opened a bag of cheesy niblets.

"Here it is!" I shouted. Then I pulled out my fantabulous new poster and showed it to her.

"Oooh—it's Serena Silvertail in the *Cindermouse* ballet," said Alice, admiring the famous ballerina. "She's soooo beautiful!"

"I specially sent away for it," I said

proudly, "to decorate our clubhouse."

I tacked the poster up on the wall, and Alice and I gazed at it.

"She's waltzing with Prince Charming at the royal wedding," I explained.

"Her dress is truly sparkly," Alice whispered dreamily, "and so is her silvery tiara."

"Don't you wish we could go to Cindermouse's wedding?" I asked, examining my scruffy school uniform. "And be the bridesmaids?"

"With special fancy dresses!" said Alice.

"And fancy slippers, too!" I added.

"Aaah," Alice and I sighed together and closed our eyes. Imagine!

Dear Diary,

This morning I was so cozy in my bed, I didn't even wake up for breakfast. In my dreams I was dancing gracefully behind a beautiful bride and holding her lacy veil as she waltzed through a garden of roses. I knew I'd seen the bride before, but I just couldn't remember her name. It didn't really matter though, because I was definitely the prettiest bridesmaid ever!

"Thank you, Angelina," whispered the bride. "You're my most very special bridesmaid."

"OUCH!" I yelped.

I woke up with a start. My baby sister, Polly, was thumping me with her grubby paws. Grrrr . . . (Polly is definitely the worst pest ever.)

"Can't you see I'm busy dreaming?" I asked.
I yanked the pillow over my head and tried to
snuggle back under the covers.

"Yummy pancakes!" Polly shrieked, bouncing
on the bed. The scrumptious smell of Mom's
blueberry pancakes wafted upstairs. My
tummy rumbled in a very unbridesmaid-like
way and my dream rose garden disappeared. I
leaped out of bed and raced down the stairs
before my silly little sister could gobble up
all the pancakes. (She is soooo greedy!)

"Good morning, girls," said Mom as Polly and I dashed madly into the kitchen. Mom heaped three humongous pancakes on my plate. Yum!

"Your mother's the best cook ever," said Dad, sitting down with a smile.

"Definitely," I agreed. My whiskers were twitching to ask Mom a big question.

"Mom, please tell me tons more about your wedding," I said. "Was it the very bestest day of your life?"

Mom smiled. "Your father was as handsome as a prince, but I was so nervous, I forgot

my bridal bouquet," she said, sipping her coffee. "Luckily, your aunt Lavender was my bridesmaid. She found the bouquet and saved the day."

Dad chuckled. "And then your handsome prince tripped over the door of the church and bumped his head," he said.

How gruesome!

"Did Aunt Lavender have a special dress?" I asked.

"The loveliest bridesmaid dress I ever saw," said Mom, pointing to the big wedding photo on the shelf. I stood on my tippy-toes (I'm soooo good at tippy-toes because of all my ballet lessons) and admired Aunt Lavender's sparkly bridesmaid dress. It was really-truly gorgeous.

"Oh, I hope-hope-hope I get to be a bridesmaid someday!" I sighed, gobbling the last pancake.

Miss Lilly was most definitely unfair at ballet school today. I was twirling in my ballet slippers, just like Cindermouse at the royal wedding, when I made a totally tiny mistake and squished William's tail . . .

"YOWEEE!" shouted William.

"Pay attention, Angelina," scolded Miss Lilly. "No daydreaming in class."

"Yes, Miss Lilly," I answered, my tail drooping. After that, I swirled and twirled

around the room very carefully, because Miss Lilly says ballerinas should ALWAYS be disciplined (and that means not twirling on other mouselings' tails). But while I was gracefully pirouetting just like Cindermouse's favorite bridesmaid, my annoying little cousin Henry hopped in front of me and I bumped into him.

Oomph. "Be careful, Henry!" I shouted.

"Mouselings must dance gracefully, my darlinks," Miss Lilly reminded us (Miss Lilly always calls us her darlinks).

"ANGELINA SQUASHED ME," Henry complained.

"I'll have a chat with Angelina after our lesson," said Miss Lilly while the horrid Pinkpaws twins snickered and pointed at me. (Ugh. They are soooo rude!)

"Angelina, darlink," said Miss Lilly when

everyone had left, "is there a problem?"

"No, Miss Lilly," I said, "but . . ."

"But what, my little mouseling?" asked Miss Lilly.

"Well, I've been dreaming about being a dancing bridesmaid in a sparkly dress, with flowers and ribbons and everything . . ." I stopped. Miss Lilly's whiskers definitely seemed to be twitching, and suddenly a question popped right into my head.

"Have you ever thought about getting married, Miss Lilly?" I asked.

"Goodness gracious, no!" exclaimed Miss Lilly, shaking her head. "You see, I never found the perfect partner, Angelina."

Dear Diary,

"What do you think, Alice?" I asked as we climbed up into the Treetop Club with our yummy snacks after ballet school. "Will Miss

Lilly ever find the perfect partner?"

"Well, she is a bit old . . ." said Alice thoughtfully, putting down her bag and munching on a handful of cheesy pops. (You have to be careful or Alice will eat them ALL!)

"But Miss Lilly could still fall in love!" I protested. Then I had the most stupendous idea ever! "Oooh! We can help her find someone—like a handsome old ballet star."

"But there aren't even any handsome *young* ballet stars in Chipping Cheddar," Alice objected, rolling her eyes. "Any more cheesy pops?"

Humph! I thought it was a truly tippety-top idea . . .

"Imagine, Alice—you'll get married some-day," I teased, passing her the very last cheesy pop (honestly!). "You'll look soooo gorgeous in your fancy wedding dress kissing the groom."

"NO WAY!" shrieked Alice, sticking out her tongue. "Anyhow, you're going to marry William Longtail," she said. "I know because he told me so."

"Horrors!" I screamed, and we both collapsed in a complete fit of the giggles.

Dear Diary,

I've been keeping an eye on Miss Lilly lately because she's acting very weird. At ballet class she lost all the sheet music, and I had to climb under the piano (ugh—it was soooo dusty!) and poke around in the lockers. Miss Quaver, the pianist, huffed and puffed until I finally found the music stuffed under Miss Lilly's handbag. Imagine!

The next day Miss Lilly was humming a silly song and didn't look where she was going.

"Zooot!" she shrieked as she toppled over Henry.

"EEEEK!" squeaked Henry. (Hahaha!)

"I'm so sorry, Henry—I'm in a bit of a tizzy these days," admitted Miss Lilly.

Then she stared dreamily out the window and forgot to watch our pliés, which was very annoying because my pliés were definitely tippety-top! At the end of class Miss Lilly blew everyone a kiss and waltzed out the door.

On the way home Alice and I couldn't stop chattering.

"I know why Miss Lilly is in such a tizzy," I declared as we skipped down Apple Tree Lane swinging our school satchels.

"Is she going on vacation to Dacovia?" Alice asked excitedly.

"No way," I replied. "I bet she has a secret boyfriend . . ."

"Really?" Alice stared at me.

"Really-truly, Alice," I said, leaping nimbly over some geraniums. "It's too bad Miss Lilly didn't ask us first, because then her boyfriend would definitely be perfect. But if we do a little spying, we can find out who it is!"

Dear Diary,

Today Alice and I were stupendous detectives—I think the best in the whole of Mouseland. We sneakily followed Miss Lilly all around the village. We had to squeeze ourselves behind mailboxes, trees, and doorways so she wouldn't see us, and we were ever so quiet, except when Alice's tummy rumbled.

"Shhh!" I warned her. "We're secret detectives now."

Then I whipped out my pen and wrote everything down.

Angelina's
Special Secret Notebook

10:02 a.m.

Miss Lilly exits ballet school and drops a very large, suspicious-looking letter in the mailbox on the Village Green.

<u>10:11 a.m.</u>

Miss Lilly goes into the Town Mouse, which is the fanciest shop in all of Chipping Cheddar. Miss Lilly stays for ages, and tries on lots of different fancy outfits and all sorts of scarves and pretty things. Miss Lilly finally comes out with three ginormous bags.

<u>11:14 a.m.</u>

Miss Lilly peers in Perfect Paws' window, the snootiest shoe and glove shop in Chipping Cheddar. Miss Lilly goes in and says she needs some "very special shoes for a very big event." Then Miss Lilly buys the most expensive shoes in the shop!

<u>12:02 p.m.</u>

Miss Lilly enters the Pink Peppermint Tea Parlor and has a long chat with Mrs. Tinsel about party cakes. "Can you make a fabulous strawberry cheesecake big enough for hundreds of guests?" Miss Lilly asks.

("OOOH!" squeaked Alice, and I had to quickly drag her away.)

Dear Diary,

Today Alice and I were very sneaky again.

After our ballet lessons Miss Lilly's telephone rang. She rushed to answer it, and she looked VERY happy.

"Please come immediately," she said. "My lessons are over."

I winked at Alice. What could be more suspicious than that?

"Let's wait and see who it is," I whispered to Alice in the changing room. Those icky

twins Priscilla and Penelope Pinkpaws almost tripped over each other trying to listen in (but this little secret was definitely for Alice's furry ears only!).

We said good-bye to Miss Lilly, but, instead of going home, we scrambled behind the hedge outside the ballet school. Alice clutched her tummy.

"I'm starving," she complained.

"Shhh! I've got some yummy licorice mouse-tails at home," I whispered. "But you mustn't make a SQUEAK now!" It wasn't totally true about the licorice mouse-tails, but at least Alice stopped squeaking. "Look, here he comes!"

Alice and I stared with wide eyes as a tall figure in a stripy suit trotted up to Miss Lilly's door with a satin box. He rang the bell and twisted his mustache nervously. Alice poked me in the ribs.

"That's Mr. Topknot from Topknot's Hat Shop," she whispered.

"Perfect for Miss Lilly," I replied. "He's got gray whiskers and he's still not married."

The door opened and Miss Lilly stepped out with a huge smile.

"What a pleasure to see you," she greeted Mr. Topknot sweetly. (Oooh, I was soooo right about Miss Lilly!)

Just then Alice's tummy rumbled horribly. Miss Lilly peered into the hedge and spied our two little tails sticking out.

Ooops.

"Hello, Miss Lilly," we said as she stared at us in surprise.

"What are you two mouselings up to?" Miss Lilly asked in a very stern voice.

"We were just tidying up your garden for you," I answered politely, holding up a twig. Miss Lilly raised her eyebrows in disbelief. It was definitely time for Alice and me to be detectives somewhere else.

"Bye, Miss Lilly," we shouted as we scampered off across the village green.

Dear Diary,

Alice and I spent all Saturday morning in the Treetop Clubhouse chattering about Miss Lilly's secret engagement.

"Just think, we can be sparkly bridesmaids at her wedding," I told Alice. "It will be like my dream come true . . ."

Alice and I got soooo excited about Miss Lilly and Mr. Topknot that we collected all our pennies and raced off to Miss Fidget's Fantastic Flower Shop. Miss Fidget absolutely detests little mouselings, but she has the prettiest flowers in all of Chipping Cheddar, and we definitely wanted the very best for Miss Lilly.

"A ginormous bouquet, please," I said, reaching up on my tippy-toes to plonk our money down on the counter.

"Too expensive for silly little mouselings," said Miss Fidget, peering down her skinny nose at me.

"We've saved all our pocket money . . ." I persisted.

"Humph," Miss Fidget snorted as she counted the pennies.

"These are on sale," she said icily as she shoved a bunch of droopy daisies across the counter.

Mom always says it's best not to argue with bad-tempered rodents so, because I am such a well-behaved mouseling, I sweetly took the daisies from Miss Fidget. Then I grabbed Alice and we raced as fast as our paws could carry us down to the village green.

I proudly rang Miss Lilly's doorbell.

"Gracious me!" said Miss Lilly when she opened the door. "What's this?"

"CONGRATULATIONS!" we shouted. Alice and I did our very best curtsies and presented Miss Lilly with the droopy bouquet.

"Darlinks, this is very kind," said Miss Lilly. "But what is the occasion?"

"YOUR ENGAGEMENT!" we continued, shouting even louder.

Miss Lilly scratched her head and looked really-truly befuddled.

"TO MR. TOPKNOT!" I added, in case she'd forgotten.

Miss Lilly burst out laughing (which was quite strange).

"Darlinks, I have some explaining to do," she said, and she invited us inside.

Dear Diary,

Miss Lilly's cottage is always warm and welcoming, with a cozy fire, a comfy sofa, and gorgeous photos of Miss Lilly twirling with the Royal Mouseland Ballet all over the walls.

"I'm afraid you've made a mistake," said Miss Lilly as she poured hot chocolate into china cups and put a plate of warm cheesy scones and currant buns on the table. "I have absolutely no intention of marrying Mr. Topknot."

My whiskers trembled and I couldn't even nibble a single scone. "But what

about all those fancy clothes you bought at the Town Mouse shop?" I blurted out. "And those gorgeous matching shoes and gloves from Perfect Paws?"

Miss Lilly looked surprised. Ooops. I forgot that Alice and I had discovered this in secret!

"You're a good detective, Angelina," Miss Lilly said, "but you shouldn't spy."

"I'm sorry, Miss Lilly," I mumbled as a tiny tear trickled down my nose.

"Tut tut. I'll solve the mystery for you," continued Miss Lilly. Then she opened Mr. Topknot's box and pulled out a gorgeous silk hat covered in all sorts of fluffy feathers.

"Oooh . . ." Alice and I sighed as Miss Lilly showed off her new hat.

"In fact, I bought this hat for the wedding of a famous friend of mine," she explained.

"Serena Silvertail!" I gasped.

"How did you know, my darlink?" asked Miss Lilly.

"I dreamed it," I said, remembering the gorgeous bride in the rose garden.

Miss Lilly smiled. "Yes, Serena Silvertail is marrying Yakov Whiskerovski," she said.

"The biggest star in the Dacovian Ballet!" I squealed.

Alice whistled and toppled off her chair.

"Yes," agreed Miss Lilly. "And they're planning a fabulous wedding at Mouseland Manor."

Alice scrambled back on her chair and sighed. "Think of all the gorgeous food and cake . . ." she said dreamily.

"Now you know why I've been busy shopping," continued Miss Lilly, patting me on the head. "I must look my best for such an important wedding."

I gazed longingly at Miss Lilly's fancy hat and wished that I could go to Serena Silvertail's wedding, too. I knew I would have to be really-truly brave about not being Miss Lilly's bridesmaid now, but I couldn't help feeling horribly sad.

Dear Diary,

Even though Miss Lilly's not-getting-married was the worst news ever, I managed to take a few sips of hot chocolate and nibble three scones for extra strength (before Alice gobbled up absolutely everything!).

"Thank you for a lovely visit," I said to Miss Lilly when there wasn't a single crumb left on our plates.

"You're very welcome, darlinks," said Miss Lilly. "Now no more spying."

Just then we heard car brakes screeching outside, and Miss Lilly peered out the window.

"Goodness me. It's Serena Silvertail!" she gasped, opening the door.

Serena Silvertail burst into the cottage with wild eyes.

"Save me, Lilly!" she cried, throwing herself into Miss Lilly's arms.

"My dear Serena," said Miss Lilly. "Whatever is the matter?"

Alice and I stared. Could this really be the sparkly ballerina on our *Cindermouse* poster?

"My wedding is a complete disaster!" sobbed Miss Silvertail.

Miss Lilly sent us off to make a cup of tea

in the kitchen while she helped poor Serena
Silvertail onto the sofa.

"I must rehearse day and night for my
next big Royal Ballet performance," sobbed
Serena Silvertail. "So there's no wedding
dress, no flowers, no bridesmaids. Yakov is
furious. The wedding is off!"

Alice and I brought Serena Silvertail a cup
of elderflower tea, and she gulped it down.
I noticed that even though she seemed the

most unhappy bride ever, Serena Silvertail
was wearing a truly ginormous diamond ring.

"Don't worry about a thing, my darlink,"
said Miss Lilly kindly. "I'll help make your
wedding day perfect."

Serena Silvertail looked up with weepy
eyes and pulled a very long roll of scribbly
paper out of her bag.

"Here's my list," she said, handing it over.

"Goodness gracious . . ." said Miss Lilly,
staring in horror.

I looked over Miss Lilly's shoulder, my
whiskers twitching with excitement. Serena
Silvertail definitely needed lots of help—
and so did Miss Lilly. I poked Alice in the
ribs and smiled ever so sweetly at Serena
Silvertail.

"Alice and I could be your helpers, too," I
said, and Alice nodded happily.

"Can you run very fast and do all my

errands?" Serena Silvertail asked us.

"Definitely," we agreed.

"Can you find a stupendous seamstress for my dress?" cried Serena Silvertail.

"My mom can sew anything!" I boasted.

"And what about bridesmaids?" Serena Silvertail continued, sniffling away.

This was it! Maybe my dream of being a bridesmaid could really-truly come true!!!

"Well . . . Alice and I could be your bridesmaids," I said, holding my breath and crossing my paws behind my back for good luck. Serena Silvertail peered thoughtfully at us.

"What a charming idea—two little bridesmaids," she said at last, looking brighter.

"YIPPEE!" I shouted.

Alice and I couldn't stop squeaking as we danced in circles around and around Miss

Lilly's sitting room. We were going to be the best bridesmaids ever!

Dear Diary,

My mom's tail shot up in surprise when I told her that Alice and I were going to be the bridesmaids at Serena Silvertail's wedding.

"Imagine that," she said, smiling at us.

"And you'll be very busy sewing," I said, "because Serena Silvertail wants you to make her wedding dress."

"What an honor," said Mom, raising her eyebrows. I could tell that Mom was secretly VERY pleased that I had been such a clever mouseling and found her such an important job as sewing Serena Silvertail's wedding dress.

"Polly be a bride-maid, too?" begged Polly, banging her cup.

"You'll have to wait until you're big like me," I explained.

Then I spied my silly little cousin Henry hiding under the table.

"WILLIAM AND I WILL BE THE BOY BRIDESMAIDS," he squeaked, popping up.

"That's ridiculous!" I shouted.

"I'm sure Miss Lilly will be delighted to have more helpers," said Mom, picking up the phone to call my ballet teacher. I could hardly believe my furry ears when Mom told me that Miss Lilly had agreed! I rushed out the door to tell Alice the terrible news.

Of course, Alice was truly horrified, so we raced off together to Mrs. Thimble's shop for licorice mouse-tails to make us feel better.

Mrs. Thimble's shop was packed with customers chattering about Serena Silvertail's wedding. Everyone in Chipping Cheddar has heard about it. Mrs. Thimble told us that tons of famous dancers and actors are invited, and guess what? The *Mouseland Gazette* will publish a huge story all about it—and my dad is the reporter.

Everything would be perfect if only my silly cousin Henry and William Longtail weren't invited. Every time I think of those two pests my whiskers start twitching madly.

"It's NOT fair!" I complained at supper. "I'm sure the boys will be on their best behavior," said Mom.

"And you'll be busy waltzing with me," said Dad proudly.

"Thanks, Dad," I said, still sulking a bit. But then I had a most stupendous idea. It was about a very special performance . . .

Dear Diary,

I phoned Alice as soon as I woke up this morning.

"Treetop Club Top Secret Meeting," I whispered.

"Wait for me!" Alice yelped. And in a flick of a mouse-tail later she was scrambling up the ladder.

"We need to give Serena Silvertail a fantabulous wedding present," I announced.

"What about a nice box of chocolates?" asked Alice, licking her lips.

"Even more fantabulous than that," I

replied. "We're going to perform a special ballet for her."

"Just you and me?" asked Alice.

"Definitely. There will be absolutely NO BOY mouselings!" I said. (Ugh. I didn't want silly William and Henry spoiling things!)

"It will be a special bridesmaid ballet."

"Will Miss Lilly help us?" asked Alice, searching for nibbles.

"No way—it has to be a secret," I told her, opening our Secret Candy Box.

"But we might get mixed up . . ." said Alice, handing out cheddar creams.

"Don't be such a worry-mouse," I said. Just then I remembered we'd promised to help Miss Lilly every day. "Ooops. Alice, we're supposed to be at Miss Lilly's cottage right now!"

When we arrived at Miss Lilly's cottage, she was busily writing more lists and talking on the phone at the same time. She definitely looked frazzled. (Mom says it isn't good manners to tell grown-ups when they look frazzled, though. How weird is that?)

"Off you go," Miss Lilly said, handing me her scribbles. Alice and I felt ever so important as we trotted around the village doing special wedding errands. But can you believe it? Everywhere we went, my annoying little cousin Henry trailed along behind us with silly William Longtail. (I simply HATE boy mouselings!)

"WE'RE WEDDING HELPERS, TOO, ANGELINA," Henry squeaked, hopping beside me.

"You are not, Henry," I said, glaring at him.

"Actually, we're Serena Silvertail's ushers," bragged William, "which means we will carry the train on Serena Silvertail's dress so it doesn't get dirty on her way down the aisle." Alice and I skipped away as fast as we could, but those two pests kept following us.

Our first stop was Pawprints's Print Shop. Mr. Pawprints proudly showed us his fanciest wedding invitation designs, and I picked out a really bright pinky-pink one, because pink is my tip-top FAVORITE color. Mr. Pawprints said it was a stupendous choice, but then he showed me a plain white design. "Perhaps Serena Silvertail would like something more traditional?" he asked.

"Hmmm . . . No, definitely the pink ones," I decided.

"Serena Silvertail is ordering two hundred pinky-pink invitations," I said, feeling very grown-up. I smiled at Alice and completely ignored the two naughty mouselings peeping over her shoulder. Grrrr . . .

Our next stop was Fidget's Fantastic Flower Shop. Henry and William followed us inside, giggling all the way. Can you imagine? Those two silly-billies wiggled their ears and stuck out their tongues the whole time I was ordering the gorgeous wedding roses. Miss

Fidget grumbled and shook her paws at them.
"I'll report you two ruffians to Constable
Crumble," she warned. That did the trick.
Before I could count ten whiskers, those
naughty mouselings scampered off with their
tails between their paws.

Dear Diary,

Miss Lilly has tons of new errands for us
every day, and she dashes off to Mouseland
Manor whenever she's not teaching ballet.
It's not so easy-peasy to get everything
ready for such a big fancy wedding, and

bridesmaids can get quite frazzled, too—even the very bestest bridesmaids like us!

Alice and I already have sore paws from trudging all over Chipping Cheddar. We deliver messages and collect packages all day long, and we mustn't forget to stop by the Beauty Mouse Spa and reserve fancy paw manicures, tail massages, and fur highlights for Serena Silvertail—she absolutely can't live without them!

Alice moans a lot because we can't stop for yummy snacks anymore, and we hardly have time to sneak off to our comfy clubhouse either. Even Mom says she's never been so frazzled. Our little cottage is crammed with silks and fabrics, ribbons, beads, and sewing boxes. Dad sighs and complains because he can't sit down anywhere, and Polly drives Mom mad dressing up in all the fancy sewing stuff (although I have to admit she sometimes looks kind of cute).

When the phone started ringing at breakfast this morning, Mom's tail definitely drooped.

"Is the wedding dress ready yet?" Serena Silvertail asked for the hundredth time. Mom had to stop everything to talk while the toast burned and the milk boiled over. (Polly and I are VERY fed up with burnt toast for breakfast!)

"WAAAAA!" shrieked Polly, banging her cup.

"Crumbs," sighed Mom, staring at the mess.

Dear Diary,

Alice and I are the busiest mouselings ever—it turns out that bridesmaids have to do absolutely EVERYTHING for the bride! How unfair is that? We're busy hopping all over Chipping Cheddar every day and then we have to sneak off to secretly rehearse our bridesmaid ballet. Even Alice, who is almost ALWAYS a cheerful mouseling, is getting her whiskers in a twist during rehearsals.

Today was definitely our worst rehearsal ever. "Remember, I'm the star and you're my partner," I told her. "At the end of the ballet I'll leap into your arms and you hold me up."

"Yikes," said Alice, looking a bit nervous (as if I'm soooo heavy!).

I twirled toward Alice and performed a graceful grand jeté, but she toppled over and we both crashed into Mom's flower bed. (Ooops. Mom won't be too happy about that.)

"Oooh," complained Alice, picking herself up.

"Practice makes perfect," I reminded her, because ballerinas never give up when they fall down—even if they do have to scrape some flower-bed mud off their tutus.

I twirled toward Alice again, but instead of catching me in her paws, Alice turned around and trotted off toward the kitchen.

"Well, practice makes my tummy rumble," she complained.

Dear Diary,

Today Mr. Pawprints finished the gorgeous pinky-pink wedding invitations that I had chosen. Miss Lilly looked at them with wide eyes and said they were "most original" (I'm sure this is a very big compliment).

Here's what the invitations say:

Miss Serena Silvertail and Mr. Yakov Whiskerovski
request the pleasure of your company
at their wedding in the rose gardens
on 22 June followed by dinner and dancing

The Mouseland Manor
Chipping Cheddar, Boltholes
Mouseland

Isn't that the most romantic thing since Swiss cheese? After we put all the stamps on, Alice and I spent all afternoon rushing to the post office and stuffing tons of the invitations into the mailbox.

Dear Diary,

Alice and I have been absolutely dying

to visit Mouseland Manor and today we had a truly BIG surprise because Yakov Whiskerovski zoomed into Chipping Cheddar in his yellow Mouserati to specially invite us! Serena Silvertail sat beside him in a silk scarf and dark glasses, waving to everyone just like a film star. She is soooo glamorous. The Mouserati screeched to a stop outside Miss Lilly's cottage and my whiskers tingled with excitement—but then Henry and William raced around the corner and jumped in beside Serena Silvertail. Imagine!

"Humph," I grumbled to Alice. "What nerve!"

"I CAN'T WAIT TO SEE MOUSELAND MANOR," squeaked my mischievous little cousin. I was sure Serena Silvertail would tell Henry off, but she smiled and tweaked his whiskers. Grrrr . . .

Alice and I had to squeeze into Miss

Lilly's shabby little mousemobile and we
bumped along in the dust behind the
gleaming Mouserati as it roared off through
the countryside with Henry and William
laughing their silly heads off.

Mouseland Manor is almost as big as the
royal palace, and just as fantabulous. The
lobby is gleaming gold, and fancy couples
were chattering together in the swanky
restaurant and lounging around the pool

while waiters brought them luscious drinks and snacks (which definitely made Alice's tummy rumble).

"This is more like it," I said to Alice as I gazed out of the golden doors and imagined myself twirling through the rose garden in my bridesmaid dress.

A uniformed doormouse rushed to help Yakov Whiskerovski and Serena Silvertail

out of the Mouserati, and a pencil-thin
hostess in a snappy suit stepped forward to
greet them.

"Welcome to Mouseland Manor," she said,
extending a silky paw. "Madame Snootfur,
at your service."

"HELLO, MY NAME IS HENRY," my
little cousin squeaked politely, but Madame
Snootfur just sniffed at him and turned
away.

Yakov Whiskerovski twitched his
whiskers nervously.

"Where's the Grand Ballroom?" he asked.
"We must have dancing!"

I nudged Alice. "See?" I whispered.
Everyone was definitely going to love our
surprise bridesmaid ballet dance!

Henry and William dashed off ahead,
while Madame Snootfur led us to the Grand
Ballroom with her nose in the air. Then she

kept going on for absolutely ages about orchestras and silver goblets and all that fancy wedding stuff. Alice pointed excitedly to all the chandeliers.

"Have you ever seen such a ginormous ballroom?" she asked.

"Perfect for our ballet," I said, imagining all the guests clapping and cheering for us.

Alice wriggled her nose doubtfully as we watched Henry and William march across the ballroom behind Yakov Whiskerovski, trying to be perfect ushers. How gruesome!

"Won't it be scary dancing at the wedding, Angelina?" asked Alice.

"Don't worry," I assured her. "Just follow me. We'll leap onstage with the orchestra just like this—" Then I twirled stupendously across the Grand Ballroom and bounded into a spectacular grand jeté.

"WATCH OUT, ANGELINA!" squeaked Henry.

Dear Diary,

After I crashed into the Mouseland Manor buffet table, Miss Lilly rushed me off to see Dr. Tuttle. I guess my grand jeté was a bit too grand. I landed upside down on top of a ginormous strawberry cheesecake and got a terrible bump on my nose. Alice said I looked like a special party pudding all covered in strawberries and cream (but she didn't giggle because she is my very bestest friend). Henry and William stared goggle-eyed while that horrid Madame Snootfur glared at me with quivering whiskers.

"Wow, that was some leap," said William.

"The Grand Ballroom is not a playground," grumbled Miss Snootfur.

Miss Lilly and Serena Silvertail peered carefully at my nose.

"Where does it hurt?" asked Miss Lilly.

"OUCH!" I yelped.

"Little bridesmaids should look before they leap," joked Serena Silvertail (hahaha) while Yakov Whiskerovski scowled at the squashed cheesecake.

"Perhaps you need a new bridesmaid," he said.

Yakov Whiskerovski's horrible words squished my heart into tiny bits and I

sobbed all the way to Dr. Tuttle's office.
When we arrived I tried to be brave even
though I was really-truly miserable.

"I was just practicing a grand jeté," I
explained while Dr. Tuttle examined my
bump.

"You little ballerinas are tougher than
soccer players," Dr. Tuttle chuckled. Then
he wrapped tons of white bandages around
my poor purple nose.

On the way home Henry scrambled in
next to me.

"YOU'RE A VERY BRAVE MOUSELING, ANGELINA," he squeaked (sometimes my little cousin can actually be quite intelligent).

Dear Diary,

Ballerinas are absolutely always professional. Even though I have a terrible purple nose bump, I've been practicing the Bridesmaid Ballet every day with Alice (after she made me promise not to do any more grand jetés). Luckily, Serena Silvertail said I could still be her bridesmaid. YIPPEE!

"Don't worry about Yakov," she added, giving me a hug. "He can be rather temperamental."

Alice whispered in my ear, "That Yakov Whiskerovski may be a tippety-top dancer, but he's not a specially kind sort of mouse like Serena Silvertail."

"He's definitely not very fond of a silly-

billy mouseling like me," I replied with
a sigh. For the first time I was getting
a teeny tiny bit nervous. What if Yakov
Whiskerovski gets temperamental about our
bridesmaid ballet?

Dear Diary,

Today is my lucky day. This morning
Dr. Tuttle took most of the bandages
off and my nose bump is definitely not so
gruesomely purple and sore anymore. I did
NOT want to perform our ballet with my
nose wrapped up like a mummy—imagine!

The other big news is that soon we'll

have our new dresses. Peach is Serena Silvertail's tip-top favorite color (although secretly I think pinky-pink would be MUCH nicer!) so Alice and I agreed on some silky peachy fabric for our dresses. My mom has been sewing madly for days. Alice and I can hardly wait! Serena Silvertail invited us to go shopping at Perfect Paws for our sparkly wedding slippers and rose flower baskets. And guess what? My cousin Henry and William Longtail were already there, grinning at themselves in the mirror. They were spruced up in bright blue usher outfits. Henry's fur was brushed and fluffy and even his whiskers were shiny—he was so clean, I hardly recognized him!

"Don't my ushers look handsome?" asked Serena Silvertail.

Alice and I giggled. They're only silly BOYS after all!

After we finished shopping, Alice and I
waved good-bye to Serena Silvertail and
skipped home together.

"Aren't we the luckiest mouselings?"
asked Alice.

"The luckiest in all of Mouseland," I
agreed, thinking about being gorgeous
bridesmaids in our own special ballet . . .

Dear Diary,

Today Serena Silvertail came specially
to Honeysuckle Cottage after her
rehearsals to try on her wedding dress.
Because Alice and I are very responsible

mouselings (and also because Mom told us we had to) we played "bridesmaids" with Polly in the sitting room while Mom helped Serena Silvertail get ready.

Finally, Serena Silvertail appeared in her fantabulous dress and gauzy veil, and she looked even prettier than my dream bride. Alice and I rushed upstairs and changed into our peachy bridesmaid dresses so Serena Silvertail could see how gorgeous we were, too.

Of course, as soon as my sister, Polly, spied my new dress and slippers, she had a terrible tantrum.

"Polly want sparkle shoes!" she wailed. "Polly want to be a bride-maid!"

"Don't cry, pet," said Mom soothingly. "I'm sure Serena Silvertail would love to have a tiny bridesmaid."

"That's not fair, Mom!" I shouted. "Polly

is WAY too little to be a bridesmaid!"

"She's such a little darling," said Serena Silvertail as tiny tears dripped off Polly's whiskers (totally on purpose!). "Polly can help scatter the rose petals."

Noooo! How could Serena Silvertail be so horrid?

"Me throw petals," declared Polly, giggling with delight.

"And you'll help your little sister,

Angelina," said Mom sternly.

I was so upset, I stomped up to my room and cried buckets. Now I'm definitely the saddest mouseling in all of Mouseland . . .

Dear Diary,

Why are some days soooo miserable?

I had to go with Mom and Polly to Furball's Fabric Emporium today because Serena Silvertail wants Polly to have a bridesmaid dress just like mine. How gruesome is that? And Polly has to have matching sparkly peach slippers, too, and her own little rose basket. She is such a copymouse!

But when we got there Polly wouldn't stand still for a moment. She scrambled away to play hide-and-seek all over Mr. Furball's shop, and poor Mom had to chase after her. Then my naughty baby sister threw herself on the floor in one of her terrible tantrums.

"WAAAAA!" she screeched.

"What a simply revolting noise," said a familiar snooty voice.

It was Mrs. Pinkpaws with Priscilla and Penelope. They stared at Polly as if she were the most disgusting little rat ever.

"Please excuse this dreadful disturbance," Mr. Furball apologized.

"Angelina's little sister is such a menace," said Priscilla, wrinkling her nose.

"Babies like her shouldn't be allowed out," agreed Penelope.

(Ugh. Aren't those Pinkpaws the most horrid mouselings ever?)

Poor Mom's whiskers were trembling as she paid the bill. I picked up howling Polly and gave her a cheesy mint from my pocket.

"My daughters were always such sweet

babies," said Mrs. Pinkpaws, eyeing Polly coldly.

"But they're definitely NOT sweet now!" I replied.

Mrs. Pinkpaws gasped, and Priscilla and Penelope stuck their tongues out at me, but I just smiled as Polly and I twirled out of Furball's Fabric Emporium.

Dear Diary,

Can you believe it? Serena Silvertail's

wedding is next week and even I am getting in a tizzy now because the Bridesmaid Ballet has to be perfect (and at the moment it is definitely NOT).

Everyone in the village is madly getting ready for all the fancy guests to arrive. The Old Goat's Cheese Inn has a bright new coat of paint, and Miss Fidget has put pots of white lilies all along the high street. Mom finally finished sewing a tiny bridesmaid outfit for Polly. I have to admit that my sister does look very sweet all dressed up, but it's hard to stop her splashing in mud puddles!

Miss Lilly gave a bridal shower party for Serena Silvertail, and her little cottage was bursting with guests. Everyone from Mrs. Thimble to Mr. Bell the old mailman was invited. Henry and William and Alice and I went early to help set out all the yummy food (greedy Alice ate tons even before the guests arrived). There was purple passion flower punch, along with Mrs. Tinsel's pretty sugar hearts, strawberry jam tarts, and cheddar fudge cake specially baked for the party. Scrumptious!

"Remember, no grand jetés on the table, Angelina darlink," Miss Lilly joked.

Hahaha.

"I hope Mrs. Tinsel makes tons of this yummy cake for the wedding," said Alice, gobbling her third huge piece.

Dear Diary,

Today, Serena Silvertail and Yakov Whiskerovski had a gruesome fight about the wedding music. Serena Silvertail said she wanted a lovely piano and romantic violins, but Yakov Whiskerovski insisted on loud drums, trumpets, and cymbals. Finally,

Yakov Whiskerovski slammed the door
and stomped off in a temper, and Serena
Silvertail collapsed sobbing on the sofa
(again!).

"What a silly-billy thing to fight about,"
Alice whispered.

"I know," I said. "Grown-ups act so weird
sometimes."

Secretly, my tummy was feeling quite
fuzzy as I imagined all the nasty things
grumpy Yakov Whiskerovski would say about
our surprise ballet. Gulp!

Miss Lilly sighed and gave Serena
Silvertail a hug.

"I'm sure he didn't mean to upset you,"
Miss Lilly said kindly.

"How can I marry such a revolting
rodent?" wailed Serena Silvertail.

A few minutes later the doorbell rang,
and William staggered into the cottage
carrying a ginormous bouquet of peachy
roses.

"Special delivery from Fidget's Fantastic

Flower Shop," William said. "With a card for Serena Silvertail."

Serena Silvertail dried her eyes on her hanky and read the pretty card.

"Darling Yakov has changed his mind and now he agrees with me about the piano and violins," she said, smelling the roses. "Isn't he adorable?"

"I guess they're getting married after all," Alice whispered in my ear.

Dear Diary,

Today is the Big Wedding Day!

Alice and I arrived at the wedding just like two fairy princesses, along with Henry and William in their blue usher suits and neatly trimmed fur. William's dad, Mr. Longtail, was our special chauffeur and drove us in a gleaming white mousemobile. We all sat up very straight next to Serena

Silvertail in her elegant wedding dress and diamond necklace and earrings—she was definitely sparkling!

Crowds were waving and cheering along the streets, and Serena Silvertail smiled at everyone while Alice and I smoothed her dress and held her bouquet. In our special bridesmaid dresses, with crowns of tiny pink rosebuds around our ears, we were definitely the prettiest bridesmaids ever! William Longtail couldn't stop grinning, and Henry kept squeaking, "YOU LOOK SO PRETTY, ANGELINA."

When the limousine arrived at Mouseland Manor, Alice and I stepped out gracefully and lifted Serena Silvertail's delicate veil. We held our heads up high and we didn't wiggle a whisker! All the fancy guests were seated in the rose garden waiting for the wedding to begin, and Serena Silvertail looked around nervously.

"Is everyone ready?" she asked.

"Polly's feeling a bit shy . . ." said Mom, holding Polly's paw.

I gave Polly a hug and whispered in her ear, "Remember, you're a big girl like me today."

"A big special girl," Polly agreed.

"You're big enough to help me throw rose petals," I continued.

"PETALS!" shouted Polly. (Sometimes I am definitely a very responsible older sister.)

The violins began to play, and Polly trotted

off beside me, happily tossing rose petals in the air. Henry and William marched along smartly together, while Alice and I did our best to be especially dainty. We carried the bride's veil with one paw and tossed petals in the air with the other—and when Alice tripped on her hem and tore her dress we paid almost absolutely no attention.

"Rats!" said Alice, but she kept on tossing lots of petals.

Yakov Whiskerovski was waiting under the arch of white roses. When he saw Serena

Silvertail coming through the garden in her lovely wedding gown, he couldn't stop staring.

"At least Yakov Whiskerovski isn't being horrid on his wedding day," I whispered to Alice. We sat down for the ceremony and didn't twitch a whisker (except when Serena Silvertail said "I do" and kissed Yakov Whiskerovski smack on the lips, which really made us giggle!).

After the wedding ceremony, all the gorgeous guests rushed off to the Grand Ballroom for dinner and dancing. Alice gazed at all the scrumptious food on the buffet table and her tail twitched madly.

"I'm going to taste absolutely everything," she said happily.

But my tummy wasn't rumbling at all—I was far too frazzled to nibble a thing. All I could think about was our surprise ballet. I wondered if it was too late to hide under the table! Everyone else was hungry though, and the dinner lasted for AGES.

When the last slice of Pink Passion wedding cake was all gobbled up, I knew our big moment had come. I told myself that I was not a scaredy-mouse, and I poked Alice in the ribs. We stood up bravely together in front of the crowd.

"As a special surprise for the bride and groom," I announced, "Alice Nimbletoes and

I will now perform our Bridesmaid Ballet."

Miss Lilly stared in amazement as Alice and I curtsied to the wedding couple, and Mom and Dad looked nervously at each other as we skipped onto the stage. But they didn't have to worry one bit, because Alice and I remembered our dance perfectly!

We twirled around the stage just like two ballet bridesmaids getting ready for the biggest wedding ever. We danced as if we were skipping through Chipping Cheddar visiting all our favorite shops and doing our special errands. We danced as we "ooohed" and "aaahed" over wedding flowers and invitations, and then we leaped across the stage and pretended we were nibbling licorice mouse-tails at Mrs. Thimble's Shop. Next, we pretended to skip across the village green and peer into the windows at Topknot's Hat Shop and Perfect Paws. Finally, we danced as if we were prancing around the rose garden behind the bride—just like the real wedding! In fact, everything went stupendously right up until it was time to do my fantabulous grand jeté. Then Alice's tail began to droop.

"Come on, Alice," I whispered. "I need you to catch me!"

At that very moment Yakov Whiskerovski

jumped out of his chair.

"Uh-oh," I whispered. "We're in BIG trouble now."

In one bound, Yakov Whiskerovski leaped onto the stage and stood beside us. Alice and I tried to scurry away, but he quickly caught us by our tails!

"I have come to join your dance," he announced with a bow.

Alice and I could not believe our furry ears. Yakov Whiskerovski is always so horrible and temperamental. How could he be acting just like Prince Charming now? Then Yakov Whiskerovski smiled and took our little paws in his big paws and we waltzed across the stage together—just the three of us. Miss Lilly stared at us goggle-eyed as Alice and I gracefully pirouetted with the Dacovia Ballet's most famous dancer.

"And now for our grand finale," said Yakov Whiskerovski. He winked at me and I twirled faster and faster before doing a truly spectacular grand jeté way up into the air. Yakov Whiskerovski caught me in his arms and lifted me up just like a feather. Cameras flashed, and for a moment, I was really-truly the most stupendous ballerina in all of Mouseland.

Dear Diary,

Today Chipping Cheddar seemed soooo quiet—and all the streets were empty. Henry, William, Alice, and I helped Miss Lilly pack tons of gifts and luggage into the yellow Mouserati for the newlyweds, and then we all said good-bye.

"We'll be back soon," said Serena Silvertail, who was now the new Mrs. Whiskerovski!

"And we'll do another ballet," promised Yakov Whiskerovski with a wink.

Then the happy couple waved good-bye to us and zoomed off in their Mouserati.

"HAPPY HONEYMOON!" we shouted as we watched them disappear.

Miss Lilly turned around with a big smile.

"I have a nice surprise for you," she said.

We skipped across the village green to Miss Lilly's cozy cottage and snuggled on her sofa with cups of hot chocolate and cheesy nutcake.

"You're on the front page," said Miss Lilly, and she showed us the *Mouseland Gazette*. There we were, two sparkly bridesmaids twirling onstage with Yakov Whiskerovski. Imagine!

I read the headline out loud: *"Chipping Cheddar's little ballerinas dance with the stars."*

"Oooh," said Alice, rolling her eyes. "So now we're stars, too!"

And that gave me a most stupendous idea.

"Let's go, Alice," I said as I dashed outside. Alice raced after me, and we did fantabulous grand jetés and pirouettes all across the village green just like star ballerinas—because practice definitely makes perfect!